To my grandchildren

Growing Up
On Purpose

ROBERT W. PARKINSON
Illustrated by Chris Martin

RESEARCH PRESS
2612 North Mattis Avenue
Champaign, Illinois 61821

Composition by Graphic World

ISBN 0-87822-239-1
Library of Congress Catalog Card Number: 84-63042

Contents

Introduction

The purpose of this book is to stimulate thoughtful discussion between children and their parents. Obviously, it will not reach its potential or prime audience without the interest and cooperation of teachers, counselors, psychologists, the clergy and other helping professionals. The simple and humane ideas expressed here are quite economically stated and will need the benefit of amplification and augmentation by way of group or family sessions in which the free flow of thought is encouraged.

The motivation for this book is to introduce to parents and children some of the oldest life-adjustment ideas which most cultures have adopted as guides for human performance. These ideas are so simple and universal that discussion should be easily forthcoming. The book was written with the assumption that, in this busy and complex world, it is possible the simplest and most basic ideas can be overlooked.

I have a granddaughter who is bright and sophisticated and this is my last opportunity to tap her on the shoulder and make sure she has not overlooked some of these basic social and thinking skills. We all want our children to be happy and productive, cooperative but tough-minded, loveable and capable of love, confident yet sensitive, and hard working yet full of the joy of life. That is no small order but one they can achieve given good and reasonable goals, the determination to reach them, and an occasional helping hand.

Bob Parkinson
Delray Beach, Florida
1985

1
About Love, Neighbors, and Yourself

The theme of this chapter is summed up in one statement—
Love Your Neighbor as Yourself. But wait a minute—hold on
there. This is not a command to jump up, rush next door, and
kiss, hug, or even shake hands with an unsuspecting neighbor.
Quite the contrary. Just read on a bit so we can at least define
terms and see what this really means.

For purposes of understanding this idea, *love* will be defined
as an *affectionate concern for the well being of others.* That involves

caring how others feel, how they are treated, and what happens to them. *Neighbor* will be defined as *anyone who exists and takes up space on this planet*. *As* will mean *similarly, the same as,* and *equally*. You will have to define *yourself,* yourself.

So, you see this idea is so simple you may wonder why we even discuss it. We discuss it here because it will encourage you to think about how life might be if we all really had as much affectionate concern for the well being of others as we had for ourselves. Think how fantastic life would be without war, stealing, murder, cheating, hate, gang fights, pollution, and all that bad stuff.

Get the picture? It would mean we'd live in a sort of equilibrium—a balance. What do you think of the idea so far? Too soft? Too impractical? Never work in this world?

Yes, it does sound a little soft but remember the *as yourself* part. You must respect yourself, too, you see. How can you respect yourself if you always lose, get a bad deal? Why, of course, you would end up not liking yourself. So, you will have to stand up for your rights *as* you stand up for the rights of others. Does that sound better?

Consider this for a minute.

- If you reject the idea of mutual concern, what will your life be like in the future?

or

- How long will it take before we destroy each other?

Bad news, right? We certainly can't afford to reject the idea of mutual respect and concern, can we? But, how can we really use the idea of loving our neighbor as ourselves in daily life? Maybe these ideas will help.

1. *Start small.* Try to have affectionate concern for the well being of *one* person. It could be a friend, mom or dad, or a troublesome brother or sister. Zero in on that one

person and think deeply about having a true concern for him or her. Let your affection flow. This allows your mind to become filled with good feelings and allows good actions to follow. Now, think about yourself and make up your mind that you will not allow that person to lower your concern for yourself. Keep it all in balance. OK?

2. *Choose a way of expressing your affection.* It can be something as simple as complimenting a friend on his looks or on something he has accomplished.

3. *Be consistent.* Try three times—at least. You may really shock the person you select the first time you act or express your concern for him or her. But, keep it up until it catches on. Few people will resist one sign of your affectionate concern for them—three times—never. And remember that your friendly concern is best expressed in little everyday things—talking, listening, laughing, and sharing ideas.

4. *Gradually try more people.* After all, if one is good, four are better. Caring is contagious, so you will spread this good feeling quickly. Perhaps, it will grow to include all of your family, friends, and teachers.

5. *Talk out any problems* (don't simmer like a pot of soup). Don't let things get out of balance. If they do, because either party has acted unkindly or thoughtlessly, talk about them openly. People will always react better to your positive concern when expressed in frank and friendly words. Again, remember the balance between neighbor and self. If you have been hurt, explain it and work it out to keep the balance. And, you never have to act like a wimp. Be friendly, frank, firm, and funny, if you can.

6. *Be ready to change and grow.* If someone has constructive help for you and it really makes sense, think about it in a positive way. You may have to make some changes, but after all that's growth and growth is life.

7. *Never, never let yourself down.* If someone is not a good subject for your concern, don't consider your efforts a

failure. And never give up your own good feeling about yourself. You know you have to love yourself if you are to be loveable.

We all wonder why the world is so messed up today. Why is there so much hate, greed, and fear? Of course, no one has the entire answer to such a complex question, but it is clear that these world problems are the exact opposite of the results of loving your neighbor as yourself. Some of us must have gotten away from the idea that we all do better when we have mutual concern for one another. But, here we are, victims of the problem, so we now must use laws and the police to protect us from one another. Perhaps we can recruit enough people to live according to our ideas so that the world will change. We can influence our own families and friends and, at least, cease to be part of the problem. It's interesting to think of all kinds of pollution as being simply the result of someone's lack

of love, care, or respect for others. Think about this and you'll be more careful about your actions in the environment—and that includes how you treat the earth and your mind.

Although the world seems in a sorry state, aren't you pleased that we do as well as we do today? There must be enough of us who share mutual concern to make life basically good. If it weren't for these people, you and I included, we'd have a jungle on our hands. Value them and yourself for that. We're the guys in the white hats!

Have you ever heard the saying *you reap what you sow?* You know, you plant petunias, you get petunias. Well, in the area of behavior, you plant hate and you get hate back. When you are greedy, for example, you put everyone on guard to the extent that they only deal with you from a position of extreme self-protection, which appears to be greed. So, plant love and get it back. Plant regard for others' rights and they'll protect yours. I hope we agree on that.

Before this section is complete, we should cover what you can do when others are abusive to you. It is sad but true that there are some very sick adults floating about. I mean mentally sick and morally sick. Discuss this with your parents and teachers after you read this. But, if any adult acts or talks to you in a way you know is not right, by sexually touching you or using foul language with you or by hurting you physically or by suggesting free drugs or the like, run (don't walk) to the nearest place of safety. The police, churches, private homes with an appropriate marker in the window, and many other places offer security. Check these out. If a parent, relative, or teacher molests you, you must report that to someone you trust. Review this with a counselor, your parents, and other people you trust. It's important.

Now, for a quick wrap-up: love others, love yourself, keep a balance, expand it, talk it out, and plant good crops.

Let's Talk It Over

1. Did you ever know a person who you just didn't like? Think about that person. What was it that you didn't like—his looks, what he said, how he acted? How could you change your feelings about that person? How could you help that person to be more appealing? Is it ever all right to hate someone? Why or why not?

2. Have you ever done something bad enough to make you dislike yourself? Did it make you feel guilty? Would it help to talk out the situation with the other person involved? What could that person do to help? What could you do?

3. Do you know someone who tries to make you or others feel guilty? Aside from ignoring the person, how could you handle someone like this?

4. Do you show the same affectionate concern for your family that you show for your friends? How do you show your affection to each group?

5. Can you point to any instances in your own life where you "reaped what you sowed"? Did you learn anything from the experience? Can you see others reaping what they have sown in their lives?

2
You Can't Do It Alone

It's rather clear that life wouldn't be too great if you were alone. Oh, of course, you could play solitaire or watch TV alone, but you surely couldn't play Ping Pong. It's interesting that Ping Pong is a good deal like life. You serve and your opponent returns it to you to do with as best you can. A good opponent can give you a lot of tricky shots to handle and that *is* everyday life.

So, you are not alone. You live in a world surrounded by people and you are part of that same environment. You are a member of a very complex social structure, each member of which has his or her own dreams, desires, and goals. How can we make sure that *each* of us will have a fair shot at these goals without stepping on each others' toes?

Let's see whether these answers make sense to you.

1. *No social, business, or personal relationship can exist successfully without a system of exchanges.* For example, you do something such as growing apples and someone else wants them enough to pay you money for them. Both people win. This is a perfect exchange.

2. *No relationship can exist successfully if one or the other partner in the exchange is punished (gets a bad deal) for his part in it.* Regardless of whether the exchange involves goods, services, or friendships, punishing a partner tends to wipe out the exchange, to make it stop. You certainly won't

sell your apples for too little money nor will the buyer pay too much for them.

3. *Social exchanges are made successful when both parties fully understand the conditions of the exchange.* No one enjoys being unpleasantly surprised. Therefore it is good to have an informal understanding when two people engage in a joint project. For example, let's say you and a friend are going to build a soapbox derby racing car. Work out the details of which tasks each person agrees to do, how expenses are to be shared, and even what color it will be and what name it will have. No big deal once you both know the set-up, but working out details is essential when you're going to share jobs such as cleaning up a yard for money or growing pumpkins for fun and profit.

4. *When exchanges go wrong, settle the issues with open and friendly talk.* Try to put things back together again. Be sure you and your partner arrange things so that each of you wins an equal amount, although it may be less than you'd expected.

5. *Courtesy is the oil which lubricates all social exchanges.* It sets a good tone for the exchange and helps each party to feel good, to win. Being discourteous or rude is a particularly harmful bit of human relations pollution which each of us can stop now and help to keep the world smiling. OK?

A person who is good at social exchanges is considered a good guy everywhere. He or she knows that it takes two to tango or whatever it is you do on the dance floor now.

Let's Talk It Over

1. Have you ever worked or played with people who are always changing the rules to suit themselves? What happens to the "balance" in the exchange between you? What can you do about the situation?

2. You agree to cut your neighbor's lawn for $4.00. When you finish, he asks you to trim the bushes as well but does not offer to pay you extra for the additional job. How would you deal with this situation? How can you balance the exchange? Would you quote a new, higher price for the next lawn mowing?

3. When you have an argument with someone, how do you handle it? Is it important that one side or the other "wins"? How can you both win?

4. When you and your friends work together on a project, what are some of the ways you decide who is to do what? What if someone doesn't do his or her share of the work? How can you make sure that everyone assumes a fair share of the work to be done?

5. How does courtesy help a relationship? What does courtesy mean to you?

3
No Free Lunch

Even though your parents don't put up a cash register in the kitchen, it doesn't mean you had a free lunch. Someone pays the bill. Sounds like another exchange, doesn't it? Someone eats—someone pays. That's it.

In the same manner, you earn your way in *every* part of life. And, one of the most important things you can earn is a good record of being responsible—trustworthy.

As we grow in all aspects of physical development, we also *can* grow in responsibility. The key to purposeful growth in responsibility is to start small and succeed and then take on some more of it. For example, your mother calls to you in the yard and asks you to turn on the oven at 4:00 because she has to go to the dentist. That's easy. You do it and you get a good meal at 6:30. But more importantly, your mother learns to trust you. Call that Step 1. Later, she may ask you to go to the store for stuff worth $8.75. She gives you a $10 bill. When you come home with the package and $1.25, she learns to trust you with money—Step 2. Little by little you build up such a good record of responsibility that your parents will trust you with the family car when you learn to drive. They are not about to part with the car if they have little trust in you. It takes many examples of well-placed trust, over time, to become a *trusted* family member.

Many young people have great anguish when they are turned down for "reasonable" requests. It's usually because of a poor record of trust over the early years. By the same token, children

learn to behave in certain ways because parents *reinforce* those desired behaviors in the early years. How can a child learn responsibility if each example of it is ignored? So, parents should notice and express their appreciation for those early steps in responsible behavior. This practice is a good example of an exchange in which both parties win. (The word reinforcement, by the way, means to make stronger.) Parents can reinforce children's behavior by noticing and praising desirable behavior. Kids can and do reinforce (strengthen) their parents' and friends' behavior in the same way. So, don't praise mom's apple pie unless you want it served often. See how that works?

Now, don't get the idea that we're all perfectly responsible all the time. We're not. It is however, one thing to *forget* to take out the garbage and another thing to not repay money you owe to a friend. It's one thing to go back on your promise to go to the movies with a friend and another thing to cheat on a test. At any rate, you know that you earn trust by your words and actions and you gain in self-respect as you grow in this regard.

You may think of responsible behavior in terms of these things:

1. Keeping your word—being reliable
2. Being honest about money knowing that "if it's not yours, it's somebody's"
3. Completing all tasks on time
4. Acting in such a way as to endanger no one's health or safety
5. Admitting your mistakes, if any, and doing better next time

Can you think of any more? Remember, earning people's trust is one of the most important things you can do for yourself and for them.

Let's Talk It Over

1. You often hear in the news of the "trusted employee" who stole money from his or her company. What can make a person do such a thing? Have you ever been fooled by someone you trusted? Have you ever fooled someone who trusted you?

2. In what ways do your parents trust you now? How would you like them to trust you in the future? How would you show an employer that you can be trusted with a responsible job? How many jobs can you think of in which people's lives depend on complete trust? How about air traffic controllers, doctors, nurses, and so on?

3. Who are the people you trust? What makes them trustworthy in your eyes? If someone violates your trust, how does that make you feel? Are you willing to trust them again?

4. Ask your parents or someone who is older how they developed responsible behavior. Did they ever let anyone down who trusted them? What happened?

4
You Really Are Special

Yeah, I know you've heard that before! Of course, you are special to your parents but not everyone feels quite *that way* about you, even though you're an OK person.

Speaking of that special you, have you any interest in history? None? Well you should because it's about you, in a way. If you exist today, you are historical tomorrow.

Did you ever hear of Julius Caesar, Moses, Cleopatra, Shakespeare, Mr. Ming (or whoever started the Ming Dynasty), or Hannibal? These historical figures lived, got their names in the pages of history, and left us to wonder if they were ever real. Yes, they were real. They were born, crawled around, ate whatever passed for baby food then, and grew up just like you. What is interesting, though, is that they were probably direct ancestors of yours. If they weren't, their friends were. In fact, every historical character contributed to the world so it would be just as it was when you were born.

Let's face one thing for sure. If you live here now, your ancestors made one heck of a sea voyage. It is said that even the original Indians came, at an early time, from Asia, and they could hardly walk that trip. So, it's likely that we all came to North and South America from elsewhere. It can therefore be said that our ancestors were very tough and brave people who could survive long periods of time bobbing about on the high seas with not a hamburger or French fry in sight.

We are fortunate to have people here from various ancient families, some black, some brown, some yellow, some red, and

an assortment of various shades of white. Skin color fades in importance when we realize the cultural, social, physical, and intellectual contributions of each group. Who these people were and what they did and contributed *is* the study of history. Look back and you realize some of our parents built pyramids, figured out how to make glass, learned to use medicine and healing arts, and even discovered how to make and play the first trombone.

The point of all this, as sketchy and incomplete as it is, is to help you realize that you are the top branch of your family tree. You are the product of untold millions of direct ancestors. You are the family treasure. You are the hope of your family and the chief architect of near future generations. *You* might think twice about selling yourself short.

In a way, you have received the gift of several million people. Let's take a look at a typical family tree. There are 14 people in your family tree only back to include your great-grandparents. Now, we can assume that there are approximately 20 years between generations so there are 4 generations every 80 years. Your great-grandparents are, therefore, approximately 80 years older than you are.

It gets to be fun to work it out further back. Let's say there are 5 generations every 100 years. There would be 10 generations every 200 years, 15 generations every 300 years, and so on. How many grandparents do you think you may have all the way back 300 years? Well, you have approximately 16,384 of them. No, that doesn't include aunts and uncles. Now, get this one! Go back 400 years and you have how many? Would you believe 524,288? Another 100 years back and you're over a million. Look at the chart on the next page and get some idea of the incredible size of your family.

| 1880 AD | 16 | great-grandparents |
| 1860 AD | 32 | great-grandparents |

Karl Marx Wrote *Communist Manifesto*

1840 AD	64	great-grandparents
1820 AD	128	great-grandparents
1800 AD	256	great-grandparents

French Revolution Started

1780 AD	512	direct ancestors
1760 AD	1,024	direct ancestors
1740 AD	2,048	direct ancestors
1720 AD	4,096	direct ancestors
1700 AD	8,192	direct ancestors

1680 AD	16,384	direct ancestors
1660 AD	32,768	direct ancestors
1640 AD	65,536	direct ancestors
1620 AD	131,072	direct ancestors
1600 AD	262,144	direct ancestors

English Beat Spanish Armada

1580 AD	524,288	direct ancestors
1560 AD	1,048,576	direct ancestors
1540 AD	2,097,152	direct ancestors
1520 AD	4,194,304	direct ancestors
1500 AD	8,388,608	direct ancestors

Columbus Discovered Western Hemisphere

1480 AD	16,777,216	direct ancestors
1460 AD	33,554,432	direct ancestors
1440 AD	67,108,864	direct ancestors
1420 AD	134,217,728	direct ancestors
1400 AD	268,435,456	direct ancestors

1380 AD	536,870,912	direct ancestors
1360 AD	1,073,741,824	direct ancestors
1340 AD	2,147,483,648	direct ancestors
1320 AD	4,294,967,296	direct ancestors
1300 AD	8,589,934,592	direct ancestors

As you look over the family tree chart, remember that each of the people indicated as just a number was, at one time, a living and breathing person. He or she was part of history.

25

Just one more thing. When you look back to year zero and before, you arrive at a figure of billions of ancestors. Now get this—*There haven't been that many people on the planet!* So now what do you say? It means, of course, that most of us are related to one another. As it is clear that we needed many billions of grandparents to produce us, and there weren't that many, it is certain that we all had many ancestors in common. That being the case, we are truly one family of mankind. Perhaps there are other interpretations, but doesn't that make sense? You think about it and figure it out!

Let's Talk It Over

1. Look at the dates on the chart in the book. What do you think an ancestor of yours might have been doing at different times? Making Beethoven's piano? Writing songs for Queen Elizabeth? Leading a silk caravan across the Sahara? Building a temple in India?

2. If you have a flair for math or have a computer, check my arithmetic. Start with yourself (1), then your parents (2), then their parents (4), and so on doubling every generation. How many ancestors do you have after 250 generations? Remember, you double the number every generation and there is a generation every 20 years or so.

3. If you feel overwhelmed by the enormous number of people behind you, realize that only your generation can move the human family ahead. What would you like you or your generation to be remembered for?

4. Imagine that you have two children, and they have two, and each of those descendents has two, and so on. How many descendents would you have by the year 3000 (given that there are 20 years between each generation)?

5

As Weird as It May Be, Your Body Is the Only One You'll Ever Get

Few of us spend a lot of time in front of a mirror admiring our bodies, but down deep inside we have to admit (secretly) that the "ole bod" isn't bad. Look at that regal chin, the broad shoulders, that shining hair, the flexibility of the back and legs, that noble face and figure. Admit it—even with a few imperfections there's nothing really all that wrong with your body.

Well, that young body is yours for keeps. Although it will grow and change, your body is going to carry you, happily or unhappily, into your seventies and eighties. The degree of happiness or unhappiness will largely depend on how you take care of it now. Ho hum! Same old stuff, huh? Yes, I guess it is but it reminds me of a friend who said, "If I'd known I was going to live so long, I'd have taken better care of myself." And he meant it!

Have you ever stayed up all night? New Year's Eve, a night supersaver plane trip with too many stops, or a "bed of nails" at summer camp? If you have, you know how you look and feel in the morning. You are weak, your eyes are bleary, you stomach doesn't feel too good, and you're slightly depressed—right? All these symptoms show that your body could not take care of all of the damage done from losing sleep. You know your body is trying to grow and also repair all of the damage which living itself causes. It can handle all this if it has time to do it—time when you slow down, rest, or sleep. The same is true of the fuel for the body. An active body needs quality food, and enough of it, to repair yesterday's wear and tear and to grow. You know all this, of course. But knowing that you want to build a good foundation for the future, you might learn more about it and take it seriously.

This will end the lecture on good eating and sleeping habits. From now on, we'll discuss some very poor health habits which you may accept or reject depending on your wit. Here is my list of destructive health habits:

1.	Cigarette Smoking	They may be debating how much harm is done by cigarettes, but no one ever argues that they are good for you.
2.	Alcohol and Drugs	Who claims to be more appealing, smarter, a better actress, athlete, mechanic, or dentist when "out of his gourd"? Only those "out of their gourds" at the time. Are they right?
3.	Weight Problems	Too bad but some people really do get too fat—and it's also too bad that fear of fat makes many people get too thin. Either excess is bad.
4.	Lack of Exercise	The magic of exercise is that it uses up enough energy to keep you slim. It also tones up all of the organs of the body and makes them work efficiently. You think more clearly and it is fun, too.

5. Reckless Activities (Such as diving into empty pools and hanging by your toes from the theatre balcony)

It's pretty hard to undo an accident. It's worse to try to live with it when you did it to yourself.

GRAMPS
R.I.P.

6. Down Beat
   Attitudes

Your body responds to your emotions and thoughts. So, stay cheerful and confident. We all get depressed from time to time but if you stay depressed too long, go to a professional helper—a psychologist, counselor, or favorite teacher.

As you guard your body and future life with careful nourishment, sleep, and avoidance of harmful habits, keep in mind that the best guarantee of a great life is *courage*. Life is tough

at all levels and you will need courage to move ahead. You do know, I hope, that life is a lot more than just getting by. So don't fear the challenges of the future. Do your best every day, with courage, remembering that the coward dies a thousand times and the brave die only once.

It might be wise to keep in mind that, sometimes, life just doesn't work out too well and problems occur. No one judges you by your problems but they do admire you when you handle them with courage. OK?

So practice good health habits, avoid bad habits, and cultivate a courageous and healthful mental outlook if you want to live happily into your eighties.

Let's Talk It Over

1. If a drug makes you feel great for 2 hours what will you feel like when the effects wear off? Is it worthwhile to feel great for 2 hours and terrible for 2 hours? What's wrong with feeling good naturally with no big ups or downs?

2. Why do you believe certain drugs are habit forming when they make you feel so bad? Can you grow to depend on them physically? How can you avoid drug dependency?

3. In a typical day, could you be dangerous to yourself or others without being aware of it? Have you ever seen unsafe bike riding by others or have you been pushed off the sidewalk by a group of kids playing around?

4. Think about the last time you solved a problem courageously. Isn't it easier to face new problems now?

6
The Quiet Time—Time to Relax and Listen

Action is exciting, invigorating, and important, but there is also a need in all our lives for a quiet time. You remember when you were a little kid and you laid on your back, outdoors, and watched the clouds and birds—all alone and quiet. Pretty nice, wasn't it. It gave you a chance to wonder.

You're not too old for that now. None of us are. We all need a quiet, secret time to be alone without a TV, radio, tape

machine, or people. Kids still do it and old people do it. It's great. We didn't take it away from you. If you don't have that now, you gave it away. And, you can have it back—now.

Scientists have found that our busy lives tend to make us tense. Tension is OK, within limits, but you don't prosper when you are too tense for too long. They also tell us that some of you in school have the same problem. We don't want you to carry that burden all your lives, do we? So, I recommend the quiet time as one great solution to tension and a help in many other ways.

Here are a few benefits of the *quiet time:*

1. Relaxation—control of stress and tension
2. Creative and original thinking
3. Problem-solving
4. Decision-making
5. Planning time
6. Confidence-building
7. Experiencing peaceful feelings

Can you see how these benefits might occur? Do the benefits sound interesting?

The first thing you will have to do is to find a private quiet-time place. Is that your room? Your backyard? A quiet park or picnic grounds? There must be some place which is quiet, safe, and secure. Next, get off your feet. Recline against a tree or on your bed or sofa and relax. Breathe deeply and let your muscles relax. The best technique I know for muscle relaxation involves the alternate tightening and relaxing of specific muscles or muscle groups. The idea is to let you feel the difference between tension and relaxation so you can detect when either occurs in your daily life. Try the tension and relaxation idea. How about starting with your hands. Tighten them real tight and hold for about 10 seconds. Feel the tension? Then let go and relax your hands completely—let them fall limp. Feel the difference? Now tighten the muscles in your arms. Hold the tension, then relax. Do this exercise until every muscle in your body feels relaxed. If you tense up again, tighten and relax your muscles until they are loose.

Finally, you'll want to free your mind from worry or tension. You might do this by focusing on a particularly pleasant place or memory. Think about somewhere you'd like to be—a warm beach, a mountain lake. Go there in your mind and let yourself relax. This will free your mind so it can simply drift.

Enjoy that good feeling for a while, trying to keep your mind blank or focused on a pleasant thing. In a few minutes, you will find your mind wandering. Perhaps a problem or decision forces its way into your mind. You may let it in, but think about it only until it causes you tension. Relax for a while and then let the decision or problem enter again if it does so naturally. But, this time you will want to state the facts about it honestly and unemotionally, all parts of it. Now, forget it! Your mind, now, knows the facts as if it were a computer. Don't worry about it. Let your computer solve it. It usually does within a few days. Your answer will come without your full awareness of how it happened. That is the quiet mind at work.

Let me stress the point that this needs practice. If at first you find it hard to relax, don't add to the problem by getting upset with yourself. After all, it's your mind, your body, and your time so let yourself go—drift with a feeling of relaxed pleasure and enjoy. You may only get a short nap out of it but that's not all bad.

Now, of course, your quiet time is great for relaxation of tension, decision-making, and problem-solving as described above. It is also a time for free and creative thinking not nec-essarily related to problems or decisions. You'll find yourself mentally rehearsing all kinds of new moves on the basketball floor, ways to swim just a little faster, a system for getting more out of your computer, the perfect theme for a school paper, how to introduce people more easily, and even how to get perfect timing in telling a joke. The list is as long as your imagination. I learned to skate by mentally rehearsing it before I stepped onto the ice. It worked.

All of this is great but how does the quiet time help your self-confidence? It can and does by setting you free from feeling like a victim. You can visualize yourself meeting new people, speaking out more in class, holding your own on the baseball team, talking to that special person you'd like to know better. Now you know how to use your quiet, creative mind for your own benefit. Now you know how to manage your active life with purposeful thought. You don't have to be unsure, awkward, or hesitant because you have solved school, social, and physical challenges with creative, relaxed thinking. You gain

confidence from a record of successes and you know how to work toward new success.

As was described in an earlier section, there are many people standing by to help you. If the daily acts of living get too confusing or if you become deeply unhappy or depressed, you probably should see one of these helpers. Ask your parents, school counselor, or religious leader about how you might find help. Just remember that getting help is not admitting defeat. Every great musician still goes to a coach for help, occasionally. Every great athlete needs help. What else are coaches for? So get on with your life, the active part and the quiet part, and know that we're all here to help each other. OK?

Let's Talk It Over

1. Some kinds of tension can be helpful. How can it help when you're at bat with the bases loaded? Or at the beginning of a 100-meter dash? Or about to go on stage in the school play?

2. When might tension hurt your performance? Did you ever get so tense before a big test that you couldn't think straight? How can you reduce your tension to help yourself do better?

3. Choose a time of day as your quiet time and practice for half an hour for a week. Keep a record or journal of how it works for you. Try problem-solving, creative thinking, and visualizing yourself succeeding at something you find hard to do. What are the results? Perhaps two or three of you can do the exercises on your own and then compare notes.

4. How can you use your quiet time to help you with your homework or with developing a skill you would like to learn?

7
How to Deal With People You Can't Deal With

Try as you will, some people end up as non-friends. There may have been people who have injured you, one way or the other, and for whom you have feelings of anger, resentment, or even hate. What do you do? Beat 'em up? Declare war? Gossip about them? No, you probably just sit and stew in your own juice, whatever that means.

Yet, you do have several options in such cases. You might resort to fisticuffs but that's not too nifty as your nose is also exposed. You might ignore them—and that's better. But, the best program is to somehow get these unhealthful emotions out of yourself. Sounds impossible or even weak willed but it's best. Let me tell you why. Medical and psychological doctors have good evidence to prove that constant strong emotions such as hate, fear, and resentment can cause physical changes in the person who has them. Here's how that works.

It is natural for the body to supply us with extra strength or speed when we really need it. So, when we hate, strong chemicals are released in us which equip us to either fight or get out of there in a hurry. The same goes for fear, of course. You've heard about the 10- or 12-year-old boy who lifted a car off his father when he was trapped under it. That's a perfect example of getting extra chemical help when you need it. You see, the fight or flight chemicals are pumped into our blood until the emergency is over.

OK, so we have a strong emotion, we get these chemicals—now what happens if we do nothing or if the emergency is not ended? You're all flooded with strong bodily chemicals and they are not used up. They simply stay in the body and do damage to it. It's like putting dynamite in a firecracker; it not only blows up, it blows everything up. Therefore, your best bet is to get rid of hate, fear, and resentment—and you can do it.

The trick is to release the emotion mentally—get rid of it. You can do this by talking it out with others or in your quiet time, or anytime really, by first realizing the emotion hurts you, not the other guy. Then, whenever the feeling appears in your thoughts, allow just a little of it to come into your mind. Take a quick peek at it and let it go—forget it. Next time the feeling appears, give it less time and get rid of it. It might help to try to see the humor in the situation. See whether or not you can laugh at something about the problem. Little by little, the experience will fade away. You know that you probably won't even remember the problem in a month. Release it—laugh—control your mind—and let it go. At least, you won't suffer any longer and will avoid future ulcers, heart attacks, and a messed up nervous system.

Your parents can help in this, perhaps. Certainly your school counselor or religious leader can help you work out even quicker and better systems. So make peace with (forgive) your enemies quickly (even if it's sometimes you). It's good for you.

One way to create a marvelous feeling between yourself, parents, and friends is to practice gratitude. You know gratitude is like applause, and no one I know can fail to be pleased when thanked or praised for a performance. You will become an expert in gratitude when you think about its function in social exchanges. Gratitude is full and sufficient payment in any social exchange which involves acts of kindness, gifts, help, or other forms of personal support. There is no need to discuss this subject further because you can clearly see how everyone benefits. Practice expressing gratitude and you may never have a non-friend or so-called enemy. You might wish to be reminded that forgiveness is always appreciated and think how good you'll feel to be rid of the burden of resentment. Enough said?

Let's Talk It Over

1. When you are handling resentment or other negative emotions in your quiet time, think of some positive things which may help you get rid of it. For example, is it the person or his or her actions you resent? How can you help the other person to change these actions? What happens to you when you forgive him or her?

2. How do you feel when you know everyone around you approves of you? How do they show this approval?

3. How do you feel about the people who approve of you? Do you like them?

4. Is it possible your approval of someone will make him or her like you? Figure out how these good feelings can be shared and kept alive.

8
What Happens Tomorrow?

Probably every parent has the same questions when you put on your coat and head for the door. Isn't it usually, "Where are you going and what are you going to do?" I thought so.

Though you can get by in that instance with "out" and "just going to mess around," you certainly can't give the same answers to yourself when you ask these questions about your future. You have to be slightly uncertain about what you will be doing in the future because you are young and, perhaps, are not sure what you'd even like to do. And, you don't know what is available and whether you can do the work. I've got good news for you. There is a good job out there for you and it's one you'll enjoy. What's the catch? Well, there are only a few catches and they are:

1. You have to *prepare* for your perfect job.
2. You will probably, pretty much, stay within a type of work which is an extension of what you like to do now.
3. You have to have some natural skills to succeed in your perfect job. (If you have fingers like sausages, you'll have a tough time being a violinist.)

That's not so bad, is it. Let's get into this a little deeper to see what we can learn.

Preparation

There are few jobs open to a person who does not read easily, spell accurately, do math handily, write easy to understand sentences, speak well, and have a good attitude about people. Specific jobs require more or less of those skills but all require a certain level. Therefore, you are *now* preparing for your future. *Every year of school you have opens up increasing opportunities.*

There was a study done in California which indicated that ninth grade performance was an excellent predictor of college success. You can see it's important to do well in school during your early years.

If you have not yet seen a guidance counselor, you soon will. You will be tested in several ways to help you determine your strengths and weaknesses. With the help of your guidance counselor and your parents and teachers, you can select courses which will keep your options open. That is, they will suggest certain subjects which are necessary if you are to attend college and prepare for a specific type of work. For example, you'll need a lot of science and mathematics if you wish to be an astronomer. They will also be able to direct you in preparing for high-paying and interesting jobs which do not require college.

Personal Interests and Skills

You have developed many more interests and skills than you may realize. However, few people are happy doing anything and everything. Gradually we develop very specific interests and, generally, interests lead to skills. Each person is different so interests and skills are, too.

Think about what interests you. Make a list of these things. Now think about what you can do well and make a list of these skills. If you have a hard time with this exercise, ask someone who knows you well to help. Often we have skills that others admire but that we hardly notice! Maybe you're good at listening to people or solving problems. Chances are you will be impressed when you look over your list.

How do these interests and skills lead to careers? Take a look at the examples below, each one based on the life of a real person.

Case 1

Interests *Elementary level*	*Skills* *Elementary level*
Gym	Good runner
Dancing	Good dancer, ballet and jazz
Talking with people	Good with people, easy to talk to, fun to be with
Listening to music	

What do you think this person does now? She's a high school dance teacher and coach of the drill team in Houston, Texas.

Case 2

Interests	*Skills*
Jr. high level	*Jr. high level*
All types of sports	Good shortstop
English	Excellent grades in English
Reading	Good typist
Likes being outdoors and in-doors equally well	Good with people, easy to talk to

This man had all the interests and skills in junior high school to be a sports writer. He's now a chief editor for *The Sporting News* in St. Louis.

Case 3

Interests	*Skills*
Jr. high level	*Jr. high level*
Sports	Good basketball player
Reading	Fast reader, fast learner
Social studies, geography	Good student and scholar
Talking and debating	Good at winning arguments
Politics	

How about this person? His life shows that a person of varied interests and skills can have several different types of careers. He has been a city planner, a packaging consultant for various companies, and is now a geography professor in a North Carolina college. So you see, you can use all your skills and interests in your career life.

Case 4

Interests	*Skills*
Elementary level	*Elementary level*
Music	Playing the trumpet
English	Good student and scholar
Reading	
Sports	Good swimmer
Being with people	Good at making friends

Here's another person who has a lot of interests and skills. What kinds of jobs do you think he has had? He is now vice president of sales in a publishing company. But he has been a music teacher and still plays the trumpet. As you can see, you are not locked in to one line of work when you have a lot of different interests and skills.

Keep your lists. Perhaps you can give them to your parents to save for you. Later in your life, it will be fun to look back and see how closely your career or jobs match your current interests and skills.

Even though you are just starting out on the road which will lead to earning a living and developing a career, you have already been acquiring skills and finding your interests. You deserve to give yourself the best start you can by getting the knowledge and training you'll need.

It is clear that in order to hear opportunity knock at your door you have to be home, awake, and prepared to answer it!

Let's Talk It Over

1. Usually we get where we're going by taking one step at a time. If you could choose any career you wanted, what would it be? What if you could have several careers, what would they be? What interests and skills do you have now that could help you reach those goals? What skills would you need to acquire?

2. It's interesting to think that you can do many things better now than you did them five years ago. What would you like to do better five years from now? Next year? Who can help you develop the skills or acquire the knowledge you would like to have?

3. Different jobs require different types of training. Do you need the same training to be an electrical engineer as you need to become an electrician? Do you need a college degree to become a beautician, a plumber, a rock and roll star?

4. After you make your list of your interests and skills, take a wild guess about what you might be doing for a career in the future.

5. Ask your parents about their early interests and skills when they were your age. Do their jobs now reflect those early abilities? What would they like to do if they had their choice? Can they still do it?

9

Being Your Own Boss—
Making Your Own Decisions

Do you enjoy making your own decisions? It can be a good feeling, especially when your choices turn out to be good ones.

The process of making decisions is an interesting one. When you think about it, each decision is actually made up of many smaller choices. It is a process of choosing between "yes" and "no" many times. For example, let's say you're going to buy a bicycle. Your thought process might be something like this:

		Yes	*No*
1.	Do I want hydraulic-mesh gears? (Please note that hydraulic-mesh gears don't exist—I just made them up for this example.)	X	
2.	If I get hydraulic-mesh gears, will they reduce the bike's speed?	X	
3.	Do I want speed above anything else?	X	
4.	Do I still want hydraulic-mesh gears?		X

So far, you have made three choices and have changed your mind once. You want speed more than anything else in this bike, so hydraulic-mesh gears are out. You go on to other choices.

5. Do I want a steel frame?	X	____
6. Is aluminum lighter?	X	____
7. Will lightness increase speed?	X	____

Now you're getting close to a final decision. You want a fast, lightweight bike. You will overlook that hydraulic-mesh, steel-frame model in the window. Instead, you'll head for the aluminum-frame speedster next to it.

Few decisions involve just one step. In many instances, your mind, like a computer, works so quickly that a decision may seem like one step. However, you have actually weighed many considerations and choices to arrive at the final decisions.

In everyday life, you can make decisions which may lead to tragic results. You don't have to be too swift to see that to go steady at 13, to smoke cigarettes, to do your Christmas shoplifting early, and to hang around with a certain group of kids are heavy decisions. Once you make them, you have to be a hero to unmake them. But, who needs a baby at 15? Who needs a lifelong cigarette habit (unless you're a laboratory rat)? Who needs a police record?

There are three important things to remember about decisions.

1. *Garbage in—garbage out.* This computer motto applies equally well to decision-making. If you get poor information to work with, you will make poor decisions.

2. *Decisions you make today can influence your life tomorrow for better or worse.* Some decisions can have far-reaching effects for your life. Choosing a career, the type of friends you have, what subjects to study, how to use your abilities—all these decisions together help build your future life.

3. *Often a decision involves saying "no" to temptation and "yes" to responsibility.* If you have to mow the lawn and your friends come by and urge you to go with them to the movies, what will you decide to do? It's a good rule of thumb to keep responsibilities uppermost in your mind. This is not to say you don't ever give in to temptation, but you have to weigh the consequences carefully. I once bought an expensive food freezer I wanted but didn't need and then found myself short of cash for necessary items. What decisions have you made—giving in to temptation—that you later regretted?

It would be helpful if we always had the chance to make decisions free from the pressure of other people. But often we must make up our minds in the midst of a group that is trying to persuade us to go along. How do you resist that kind of pressure, especially when you want to be liked by the group and be part of what they do? I admit, that's a heavy pressure to resist! But sometimes you will need to say "no" when the group wants you to say "yes." As hard as it may be, you may need to go your own way in order to maintain your self-respect. Here are some ideas to keep in mind that might help you make these hard decisions in the future.

1. *When you are pushed by an individual or group to agree to something you don't want to do, keep in mind that people usually have short memories whether you say yes or no.* Most of the time the group won't remember your decision for more than a day or two. In fact, sometimes the pressure you feel about a decision is based more on what you *think* the group will feel about you than what they actually *do* feel.

2. *When you are pressured to make a decision against your will, chances are the only reaction you'll get for saying "no" is a mild verbal put down or another minute or two of sales talk.* If you stick by your decision, the other person or the group will usually accept it. It's against the law to kidnap you, you know.

3. *Saying "no" gets easier the second and third time around.* Practice makes it easier. Discovering what *you* want or think is part of discovering who you are. It's one of the most important discoveries you can make. If you let others dictate what you like or what you think, you'll know who *they* are but you won't get to know *yourself.*

4. *When you learn to say "no," you might be surprised to find that your decision is contagious.* Sometimes others in the

group are hesitant to go against the crowd. If you make your decision and stick by it, they will join you. More than once this has happened to me, and I know it works.

You will be making decisions all your life. It makes a great deal of difference if you pilot your ship or simply drift with the tide. Practicing decision-making now can prepare you for some of the hard decisions you'll need to make later on in life. Whatever direction you go, it's your decision.

Let's Talk It Over

1. Think about the "garbage-in, garbage-out" idea. Where do you get the information you use to make a decision? Do you ask friends, your parents, your brother or sister? Do you find facts or ideas yourself? How does the quality of information affect your decision?

2. Many decisions are made for us—how fast you can drive, what age you can drink, how much tax your parents pay, and how loud you can play your radio or cassette player in public. If you were making some of these decisions, what limits would you set? How would you go about choosing these limits? What information would you need?

3. Have you ever made a decision that went against what the group wanted? How did it work out? Have you ever said "yes" against your better judgment? What happened? How did you feel? How can you say "no" to persuasion and still remain part of the group?

4. Ask your parents or teachers about decisions they have made. Have they ever gone against a group they were in? How did it turn out? How do they go about making difficult decisions?

10
Purposeful, Independent Thinking

Let's hope you have enjoyed this little book so far. As you know, we have discussed ways in which certain behaviors and attitudes can make your life more pleasant and productive. Now, we're going to wind up this book by discussing the most important topic of all—your mind. Yeah, I know your brain is a bunch of little gray cells, but we're interested in what you allow to enter it, what you believe, how you test your beliefs, and what you accept as truth.

The world runs on communication—spoken and written words, pictures, and all sorts of visual and auditory information. What do you suppose the reason is for all this communication? It is to convey or send out impressions to your mind which the sender hopes you will accept and use. Even a hungry baby sends out these very purposeful signals.

Now just think for a minute about all the signals you receive every day. Of course, there are the TV, radio, movies and plays, music, political speeches, advertisements of all kinds, facial expressions, physical actions, screams, smoke escaping from a building, and you take it from there. They all do, in fact, send you signals, don't they?

Most of the signals you receive are easy to handle. You smile back at a smile, call the fire department in case of fire, and avoid a guy with an angry expression. But what do you do with signals which are sent out for one purpose—to influence your mind, to get your consent, or to sell you something? If

you took in and accepted *all* of these messages, you'd have 30 brands of toothpaste, you'd vote for both candidates, and you would be for and against every issue of the day. Right? So, sooner or later, you will have to make up your mind one way or the other.

Of course, once you make up your mind, you can always change it if you find new evidence or facts. So, to develop a workable system for deciding which messages you will accept and act on, think about these points:

1. *Watch out for arguments that label any group of people or things as all good, all bad, or all anything.* These arguments are usually opinions and are not based on facts. For example, *all* my ideas are good, *all* Albanians have large noses, *all* Irishmen are quick tempered. You see these are purely opinions. However, it is a *fact* that water is composed of hydrogen and oxygen. See the difference?

2. *Watch out for arguments that draw false conclusions from true statements.* For example, friends are expected to help each other with school work—and you are a friend of mine—therefore you can be expected to write my theme for me. The key word in this proposition is *help*. Sure, help is fine but what do I learn if you do the work?

3. *Watch out for conclusions which sound reasonable but are false because they are based on false arguments.* For example, physical agility decreases rapidly after age 35 and the most important asset in flying airplanes is a high level of physical agility. Therefore, no airline pilot should be over 45 or 50 years of age. You see that sounds pretty much okay, but with all of the navigation and safety instruments and given the incredible size of modern airplanes, the most important factors in piloting an airplane are experience, good judgment, and mental alertness, not quickness of movement.

4. *Watch out for arguments that use strong emotions, rather than facts, to convince you.* Chances are that superemotional arguments are weak on facts or else why use the

phony emotions. After all, that's hard work. So watch out for the friend who tells you what *fantastic fun* it is to camp out in a dismal swamp. It may be true but check out the facts before you decide to sleep with alligators.

5. *Watch out for presentations or statements which use semi-facts to convince you.* Just because Gloria Jones is for candidate Smith doesn't mean that candidate Smith is the best choice. It *is* a *fact* that Gloria Jones is for candidate Smith. Whether or not Smith is a good candidate depends on many other facts.

6. *Test the facts you are given against your own experience or the experience and knowledge of others.* Everyone tends to use "facts" for his or her own purpose. Two aspirins may have the same ingredients as shown by laboratory tests, but each company will "prove" its brand is better than the others. In many types of persuasive communication, "facts" are often bent for the advantage of the sender and what is presented to you is often a conclusion based on half facts—or none at all.

7. *Watch out for arguments that attempt to make you do something illegal, immoral, or against your better judgment and promise big profits in the end.* Many a con artist now has a room with a view in the state prison. People who play on our natural temptations to get rich quick actually believe we deserve to be cheated and sure enough we are. Remember—you reap what you sow!

8. *Watch out for arguments that seem attractive but are really unrealistic.* For example, when you learn to drive in high school and have a part-time job at the fast-food restaurant, you may want to buy a car. The first used car salesman you visit will probably have a cream puff just

right for you for only $300. You can drive the car out for just $100 cash and payments of just $50 a month. Now, you make $100 a month and need records, school supplies, clothes, and date money which runs close to $75 a month. Can you really afford the car?

9. *Don't allow yourself to be pressured into making a decision too fast.* Salespeople are often trained to get an answer from a customer on the spot. If the salesperson really wants to make the sale, you should be allowed time to think it over. The same holds true for other types of decisions. Of course, you'll test the arguments in light of your experience but don't rush. Cool it—take your time. Otherwise you too may own a 10-year subscription to the Quilt and Doily Journal.

You will learn a great deal about independent thinking as you gather more knowledge and experience. There are many courses in decision-making and logic offered in high school and college that can help you develop your own judgment. Older people can also give you the benefit of their experience, knowledge, and mistakes. Knowing how to sort the false messages from the good ones can help you protect yourself. You will be able to make up your own mind about what you like and dislike, what is good and bad for you, what is helpful and harmful.

You'll be getting to know your own mind and learning how to be your own boss—and that's what growing up on purpose is all about!

Let's Talk It Over

1. How can we sift what is true from what is false in the messages we receive? Have you ever accepted a message as true only to find later that the "facts" were not accurate?

2. Advertisements are meant to persuade you to buy products or services. Over the next few days, watch or listen to several commercials. What are they trying to tell you about their products? What do they say about their competitors? What do they claim their products will do for you? On the basis of the information in the commercials, would you buy the products or services? Why or why not?

3. Make a list of things you believe to be true—for example, one rock group is better than another, tall people have an advantage in the world, boys (or girls) are better drivers. Why do you believe the items on your list are true? In what way can you prove that?

4. Ask your parents or someone older if they were ever pressured into buying something they didn't really need. How were they persuaded? What did they learn from the experience?

Closing

When you read this section, you have either just finished the book or you read books backwards. If you are at the end of this study, it might be helpful to summarize the ideas we have covered.

First, we have seen that basically we all want and need the same things—to do things well and to be appreciated and accepted by others. Expressing mutual concern and caring for one another is one way in which we can achieve these goals. A balance of self-love and love of others can help guarantee our best chance for happiness.

Second, we saw how our lives mix with other lives into a vast and complex social environment. There are some basic

guidelines that can help us live in harmony with one another and still remain independent—a balance, again, of ourselves and others. Part of that balance is learning to accept responsibilities and to earn the trust of others. Whenever these guidelines are forgotten or violated, human relations suffer. We also talked about your astounding family tree that reaches back through the centuries. We all share many ancestors in common, which makes differences based on skin color, race, and creed seem much less important.

Third, we took a look at that marvelous creation, your body. Even though you might like to make some changes in it, your body is still pretty amazing. We talked about good health care, quiet time, and how to get rid of hate, fear, and resentment. Remember that you are building the foundation of your health now. You can have a long, enjoyable life ahead of you if you treat yourself well.

Fourth, we discussed the world of work that lies ahead of you, and some of the ways you are already preparing for the future. Your future is really a great adventure, so relax and take one step at a time.

Finally, we talked about learning to make your own decisions and evaluating the messages you receive. We closed the book with some ideas about how to do straight thinking so you won't be taken in by phony arguments or high-pressure tactics. Remember, you can be much more than you think, *if you think!*

Talk over the ideas in this book with your parents, friends, teachers, counselors, or others that you like and trust. Ask about their experiences, and share yours with them. Your life, with all its ups and downs, can be a wonderful trip. I envy you. Good luck!

About the Author

After a baccalaureate degree in psychology in 1942 from Knox College (Illinois), four years in the Army Air Corps chiefly as a trom-bonist, and two years of graduate study in psychology at the University of Kansas, Bob Parkinson entered the publishing field. He has worked with various firms as sales representative, college-level acquisitions editor, and divisional manager. In 1969, he founded Research Press Company. In that time he has been closely associated with a variety of human services professionals and those they serve.

Mr. Parkinson wrote this book for young people quite by accident. He became interested in how various cultures acquired their social and ethical value systems. He observed that while we may believe that we are motivated by such abstractions as Truth, Love, Beauty, and Justice, it is difficult to define them except as they are tied to certain behaviors. If that is indeed a correct assumption, the building blocks of a culture must be basic action-centered concepts or behaviors. This book, then, evolved from Mr. Parkinson's attempt to pinpoint certain of those behaviors which would be understandable to young people who are just entering the social world. "Perhaps it's never too late to help young persons think about their place in the social world and the complexities of human interactions. I surely hope they will take this effort seriously enough to argue with me at least, or go far beyond me at best." Toward that end, this book is offered.

Mr. Parkinson has three children and two grandchildren. He and his wife, Ann, live in Delray Beach, Florida.